We're Kiwi and Pear!
We like to go

around the world
with bags in tow.

We ride a cable car
all around town,

then we watch
the sun go down.

We climb the steps
   at mayan sites.
At fiesta time
   we dance all night.

We paddle down
the Amazon,

then hike the Andes
with backpacks on.

At the south pole
we cruise by ship.
We laugh when penguins
dive and dip.

S.S. KIWI AND PEAR

We take a Big Apple ferry ride.
The Statue of Liberty is New York's pride.

MISS LIBERTY

Tucked in a phone booth
in LONDON TOWN,
we call for a taxi
to drive us around.

All over Paris
     we bike for an hour.
Then we climb
     the Eiffel Tower.

At the canal
  we hop into a boat.
When you're in Venice,
  it's nice just to float.

On a sunny day
we sail the Nile,
then take a camel
ride in style.

On safari in Kenya,
we ride in a jeep.

Under a tree
a lion's asleep.

JMW 610

The Great Barrier Reef
is lots of fun.
We snorkel awhile,
then sit in the sun.

Posing for pictures
at the Taj Mahal,

We ride an elephant
and have a ball.

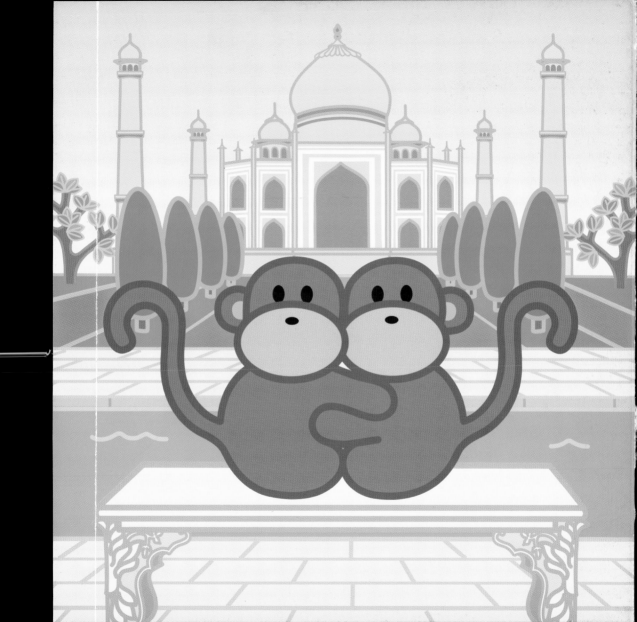

We hike up and down
china's Great Wall,
then duck into a tower
as rain starts to fall.

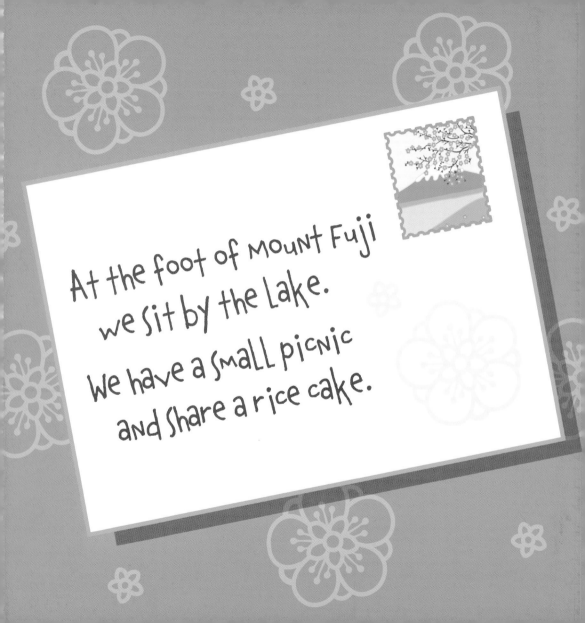

At the foot of Mount Fuji
we sit by the lake.
We have a small picnic
and share a rice cake.

We visit Red Square
on a snowy day,
then go to the theater
to watch the ballet.

We blast into space
in a rocket ship,
then float together
on an outer space trip.

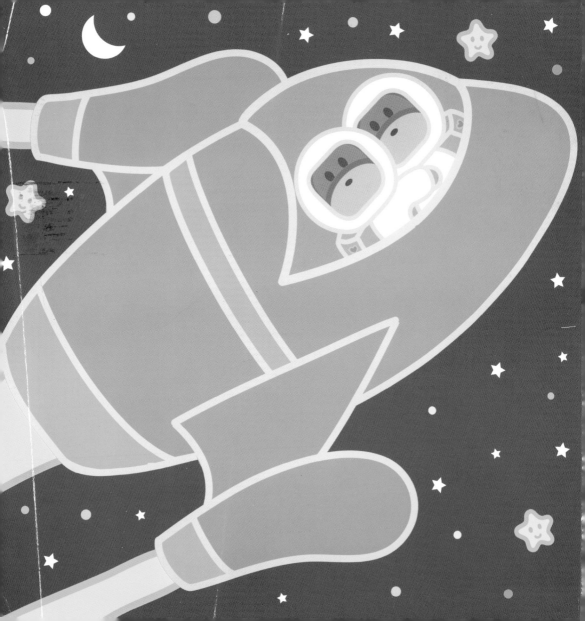